TH____EAKS

STEWART FALLS

LONE PEAK

CAVE

UNCLE BUD'S PARK

JUMPER'S HOLE

POKEY'S PLACE

CHERRY CREEK

THE MEADOW

LILY'S BURROW

MS. HOOT'S GARDEN

TAGALONG ALLIE'S BURROW

Sophie
and the
Perfect
Poem

To my daughter Beth, steady, accepting,
and a friend to everyone.
—Sean Covey

For my brother, Jeff
—Stacy Curtis

SIMON & SCHUSTER BOOKS FOR YOUNG READERS
An imprint of Simon & Schuster Children's Publishing Division
1230 Avenue of the Americas, New York, New York 10020
SIMON & SCHUSTER BOOKS FOR YOUNG READERS is a trademark of Simon & Schuster, Inc.
For information about special discounts for bulk purchases, please contact Simon & Schuster Special Sales at
1-866-506-1949 or business@simonandschuster.com.
The Simon & Schuster Speakers Bureau can bring authors to your live event. For more information or to book an
event, contact the Simon & Schuster Speakers Bureau at 1-866-248-3049 or visit our website at
www.simonspeakers.com.
Book design by Laurent Linn
The text for this book is set in Montara Gothic.
The illustrations for this book are rendered in pencil and watercolor.
Manufactured in China
Manf code 0813 SCP
2 4 6 8 10 9 7 5 3 1
Library of Congress Cataloging-in-Publication Data
Covey, Sean.
Sophie and the perfect poem / Sean Covey ; illustrated by Stacy Curtis.
— 1st ed.
p. cm. — (The 7 habits of happy kids ; [6])
Summary: Ms. Hoot assigns Sophie and Biff as partners to write a poem,
then encourages Sophie to open her eyes to the possibility that Biff is
not as mean and scary as he seems and has some good ideas, too.
ISBN 978-1-4424-7651-6 (hardcover : alk. paper)
[1. Cooperativeness—Fiction. 2. Schools—Fiction. 3. Squirrels—Fiction.
4. Animals—Fiction.] I. Curtis, Stacy, ill. II. Title.
PZ7.C8343Sop 2014
[E]—dc23   2012041833
ISBN 978-1-4424-7652-3 (eBook)

Sophie
and the
Perfect
Poem

SEAN COVEY

Illustrated by Stacy Curtis

SIMON & SCHUSTER BOOKS FOR YOUNG READERS

New York London Toronto Sydney New Delhi

At school one day, Ms. Hoot said, "Class, I am going to pair you up with a partner and have you write a poem to share with the class in one week."

I hope that I get Lily as my partner, Sophie thought.

"Lily, you'll be with Pokey. Allie, you'll work with

Sammy, and Goob and Jumper will be together.

"And Sophie and Biff," said Ms. Hoot.

Sophie couldn't believe it. She didn't want to be
partners with Biff. Biff was mean and scary.

"Geez, Sophie. Sowwy you got Biff," said Tagalong Allie.

"Yeah," said Jumper. "That's a real bummer."

"I'm probably going to have to write it all by myself,"

said Sophie. "It has to be perfect."

The next day, Ms. Hoot gave everyone time to meet with their partners. Sophie and Biff got together in the corner by the fish tank.

"I think we should write a poem about the sun, moon, and stars," said Sophie.

"That's dumb," said Biff. "I think we should write a poem about trees, wind, and water."

Sophie sighed. This was going to be even harder than she thought.

Sophie decided to talk with Ms. Hoot.

"Can I please get a different partner? Biff isn't very nice
and he doesn't have any respectable ideas."

"Oh, my dear Sophie. If you get to know him, you'll find that Biff is really nice and he has lots of good ideas, just like you," said Ms. Hoot. "I'm sure you two can come up with a poem that you both are proud of. Just open your eyes."

Sophie agreed that she would try.

So Biff and Sophie started working on their poem.

"What do you like about trees?" asked Sophie.

"You can use them to make a beaver dam. My dad made one that took him six months and I got to help."

"That's cool," said Sophie.

"I also like the sun, moon, stars, and all that stuff, too," said Biff.

"You do?" said Sophie. "Well, maybe we could put our ideas together."

They got to work.

Over the next few days, Sophie and Biff hardly took a break.

The big day had arrived. It was time for everyone
to share their poems. Goob and Jumper got up in
front of the class and read their poem first.

"Our poem is called 'Bugs and Basketballs.' Here goes," said Goob.

Basketballs and little bugs
Everywhere you look.
Little bugs and basketballs
See them in a book.
If I had an ant
I would hide him in a plant.
If I had a ball
I would bounce it off a wall.
That would be real fun
Too bad this poem is done.

"Well," said Ms. Hoot. "That was . . . ummm . . . interesting."

Next up were Sophie and Biff. Biff nervously read
their poem, as Sophie stood proudly by.

"Our poem is called 'Open Your Eyes.'"

I opened my eyes and what did I see?
The sun, the moon, the stars, the trees.
I opened my ears and what did I hear?
A gentle breeze on water clear.
I opened my heart and what did I find?
An awesome new friend and a wonderful time.

Biff and Sophie gave each other a high five and the whole class cheered.

"Well, ruffle my feathers!" said Ms. Hoot. "That was perfect!"

"Wow, Sophie. Your poem was weally, weally good,"

said Tagalong Allie. "I guess Biff wasn't so bad, huh?"

"Hey, everyone, let's play some soccer!" Jumper called.

"Great!" Sophie said. "Biff, are you coming?"

PARENTS' CORNER

HABIT ⑥ —Synergize: *Together Is Better*

SYNERGY IS WHEN TWO OR MORE PEOPLE WORK TOGETHER TO CREATE SOMETHING BETTER than either could alone, just like Sophie and Biff did when they wrote their poem. Unlike compromise, where 1+1 equals 1 ½, with synergy, 1 + 1 can equal 3 or more. It's not your way or my way but a better way, a higher way. Builders know all about this. They know that one two-by-four beam can support 607 pounds, but two two-by-fours nailed together can support not just 1,214 pounds (which is what you'd expect), but a whopping 4,878 pounds! So it is with us. We can do so much more together than we can alone.

The fact is, we are all different in so many ways, and that's a wonderful thing. As Dr. Seuss put it, "Some are fast. And some are slow. Some are high. And some are low. Not one of them is like another. Don't ask us why. Go ask your mother." And if we can learn to value our differences and see them as an advantage, instead of being afraid of them and seeing them as obstacles, we will get so much more accomplished—at home and work, in our marriages and friendships, or wherever life may lead.

In this story, point out how Sophie and the gang judged Biff without really knowing him. They thought he was mean and scary. In reality, he was just different. But once Sophie opened her eyes and really got to know Biff and valued his strengths, and Biff did the same with Sophie, good things happened.

So the next time someone disagrees with you, say, "That's good. I'm glad you see it differently."

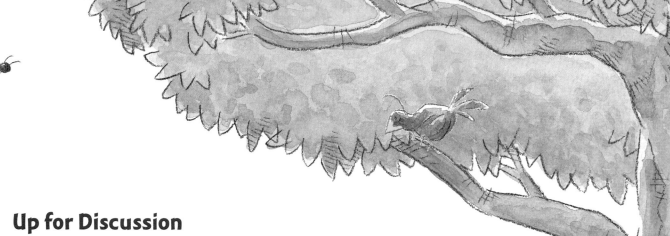

Up for Discussion

1. Why didn't Sophie want to work with Biff?
2. What did Sophie want to include in the poem? What did Biff want?
3. How did they work together to come up with the perfect poem?
4. How did the rest of the 7 Oaks gang treat Biff in the end? Why?
5. What does teamwork mean? Why is it important to include others?

Baby Steps

1. The next time you're at school, talk to someone in your class you wouldn't normally talk to.
2. Have you ever been left out? Talk with your mom and dad about how that made you feel.
3. Work with another person to write a poem or draw a picture.
4. Plan an outing with your family and include everyone's best ideas.
5. Talk to your mom and dad about not judging people. Discuss why differences are good.